The Boxcar Children Mysteries

THE BOXCAR CHILDREN
SURPRISE ISLAND
THE YELLOW HOUSE MYSTERY
MYSTERY RANCH
MIKE'S MYSTERY
BLUE BAY MYSTERY
THE WOODSHED MYSTERY
THE LIGHTHOUSE MYSTERY
MOUNTAIN TOP MYSTERY
SCHOOLHOUSE MYSTERY
CABOOSE MYSTERY
HOUSEBOAT MYSTERY
SNOWBOUND MYSTERY
TREE HOUSE MYSTERY
BICYCLE MYSTERY
MYSTERY IN THE SAND
MYSTERY BEHIND THE WALL
BUS STATION MYSTERY
BENNY UNCOVERS A MYSTERY
THE HAUNTED CABIN
   MYSTERY
THE DESERTED LIBRARY
   MYSTERY
THE ANIMAL SHELTER
   MYSTERY
THE OLD MOTEL MYSTERY
THE MYSTERY OF THE HIDDEN
   PAINTING
THE AMUSEMENT PARK
   MYSTERY
THE MYSTERY OF THE MIXED-
   UP ZOO

THE CAMP-OUT MYSTERY
THE MYSTERY GIRL
THE MYSTERY CRUISE
THE DISAPPEARING FRIEND
   MYSTERY
THE MYSTERY OF THE SINGING
   GHOST
MYSTERY IN THE SNOW
THE PIZZA MYSTERY
THE MYSTERY HORSE
THE MYSTERY AT THE DOG
   SHOW
THE CASTLE MYSTERY
THE MYSTERY OF THE LOST
   VILLAGE
THE MYSTERY ON THE ICE
THE MYSTERY OF THE
   PURPLE POOL
THE GHOST SHIP MYSTERY
THE MYSTERY IN
   WASHINGTON, DC
THE CANOE TRIP MYSTERY
THE MYSTERY OF THE HIDDEN
   BEACH
THE MYSTERY OF THE MISSING
   CAT
THE MYSTERY AT SNOWFLAKE
   INN
THE MYSTERY ON STAGE
THE DINOSAUR MYSTERY
THE MYSTERY OF THE STOLEN
   MUSIC

The Mystery at the Ball Park

The Chocolate Sundae Mystery

The Mystery of the Hot Air Balloon

The Mystery Bookstore

The Pilgrim Village Mystery

The Mystery of the Stolen Boxcar

Mystery in the Cave

The Mystery on the Train

The Mystery at the Fair

The Mystery of the Lost Mine

The Guide Dog Mystery

The Hurricane Mystery

The Pet Shop Mystery

The Mystery of the Secret Message

The Firehouse Mystery

The Mystery in San Francisco

The Niagara Falls Mystery

The Mystery at the Alamo

The Outer Space Mystery

The Soccer Mystery

The Mystery in the Old Attic

The Growling Bear Mystery

The Mystery of the Lake Monster

The Mystery at Peacock Hall

The Windy City Mystery

The Black Pearl Mystery

The Cereal Box Mystery

The Panther Mystery

The Mystery of the Queen's Jewels

The Stolen Sword Mystery

The Basketball Mystery

The Movie Star Mystery

The Mystery of the Pirate's Map

The Ghost Town Mystery

The Mystery of the Black Raven

The Mystery in the Mall

The Mystery in New York

The Gymnastics Mystery

The Poison Frog Mystery

The Mystery of the Empty Safe

The Home Run Mystery

The Great Bicycle Race Mystery

The Mystery in the Computer Game

THE MYSTERY IN THE COMPUTER GAME

created by
GERTRUDE CHANDLER WARNER

Illustrated by Hodges Soileau

SCHOLASTIC INC.
New York Toronto London Auckland Sydney
Mexico City New Delhi Hong Kong

ISBN 0-439-12960-5

12 11 10 9 8 7 6 5 4 3 2 1   0 1 2 3 4/0

Printed in the U.S.A.   40
First Scholastic printing, October 2000

Contents

CHAPTER   PAGE

1. Trolls and Trouble   1
2. A New Quest   15
3. Eavesdropping   29
4. Whispers at Breakfast   39
5. A Lunchtime Mystery   55
6. Wrong Information   63
7. The Computer Talks Back   74
8. A Mysterious Fountain   83
9. Listening In   93
10. The Aldens Set a Trap   102

THE MYSTERY IN THE
COMPUTER GAME

CHAPTER 1

Trolls and Trouble

One rainy day, the third one in a row, the four Alden children and their cousin, Soo Lee, gathered around the family computer. They were playing *Ringmaster*, a game Grandfather Alden had given to Henry for his fourteenth birthday.

"I'm stuck," ten-year-old Violet said. "I made all the trolls disappear except one."

"Can Soo Lee and I try?" Benny asked.

He was six and already an expert on the computer. Soo Lee was pretty good, too, and *Ringmaster* was their favorite game.

"Know what?" Benny said to Soo Lee. "When it's our turn, let's give the troll an apple from the boy's pack. Maybe he'll go away. Then the little kids can get to the waterfall."

Violet lifted her hand from the computer mouse. "Okay, you try, Benny. I'm going out to the porch to play checkers with Grandfather."

Benny sat down at the computer. "We know what to do. Right, Soo Lee?"

Soo Lee nodded. "That troll is scary," she said, "but the kids are just like us."

"And the Magician is just like Grandfather," Benny added. "And their dog, Tracker, is just like our dog, Watch."

Watch heard his name from where he lay under the computer desk. He thumped his tail against the wooden floor to let everyone know he was listening.

Twelve-year-old Jessie pushed a stray curl back from Benny's forehead so he could see better. "That's why Grandfather bought us *Ringmaster*," she explained. "There are five children and a dog in the game. They all live by themselves out in the woods. They have to solve mysteries to find the magic ring."

"We're always solving mysteries, too," Benny said. "And we find things, too, and not just on a computer. Only we don't live in a boxcar in the woods anymore but right here in Grandfather's house."

Benny and Soo Lee went back to *Ringmaster*. Henry and Jessie looked on. They let the younger children figure out the game by themselves.

The computer made a *dub-dub* sound.

Benny slowly read aloud the pop-up message over the troll's head:

> *"I thank you now for feeding me.*
> *Travel forward,*
> *But watch out for the tree."*

"The apple worked, Benny. The troll is gone," Jessie said.

"Hey, that reminds me," Benny said. "I'm hungry."

Henry laughed. "Even computer food makes you hungry."

Luckily for Benny, Mrs. McGregor, the family's housekeeper, showed up just in time. She held out a plate of her famous chocolate chip cookies. "How about a snack? You children were so caught up in your game, you didn't even notice I was baking cookies."

"How come you didn't ask Soo Lee and me to help?" Benny asked.

Mrs. McGregor held out the plate. "I usually don't *have* to ask. The minute you hear me clanking my baking bowls, you're right there. But ever since your grandfather brought that game home, I've lost all my kitchen helpers!"

Henry took a warm, gooey cookie. "Not anymore, Mrs. McGregor. We've almost finished the whole *Ringmaster* game. It's fun, but not as much fun as making cookies and eating them."

Mrs. McGregor handed him the plate. "Why don't you bring the rest of these out to Violet and your grandfather. He was getting pretty lonesome out there. Goodness, you children used to play checkers with him for hours on end not so long ago."

The rain was still falling when everyone joined Violet and Grandfather on the porch. Violet jumped one of her red pieces right over two of Mr. Alden's black pieces.

"You won again!" Mr. Alden said. "Have you been practicing computer checkers behind my back?"

Violet grinned. "Sometimes, Grandfather," she confessed. "But I like playing with you much better than playing on any old computer."

Everyone noticed Grandfather had an extra twinkle in his eye. This usually meant something special was about to happen. The children didn't have to wait long to find out what it was.

Grandfather settled back in his chair. "Speaking of old computers, when I bought *Ringmaster* for Henry's birthday, the salesperson told me our computer is too old to run *Ringmaster II*."

"*Ringmaster II*?" Henry said. "That's not

out yet, Grandfather. At Computer City, people have to put their names on a long list to get it when it goes on sale. The company that makes it keeps delaying the date."

"Well, I have some good news about that," Grandfather said. "We don't have to wait until *Ringmaster II* goes on sale. And we don't even have to buy a new computer, either. The nephew of my friend John Romer is the founder of QuestMaster. The company is replacing all their computers. They're donating most of their old ones to a school. The good news is that John's nephew, Charles, set aside one for you children when he heard we needed one with more power."

"QuestMaster," Jessie said. "Isn't that the company that designed *Ringmaster*?"

"Exactly right," Grandfather said. "They've moved their headquarters out near the university, not far from Greenfield. It seems they've been having problems with the new game. They've hired some students and engineers from the university to help them work out the bugs."

Soo Lee looked up at Grandfather. "Are there bugs inside our computer? I saw trolls but no bugs."

"The bugs Grandfather is talking about are little problems," Henry said. "Like when something bugs us."

Mr. Alden had more good news. "One other thing. The company likes to try out all their games with real players. You children have been invited to test out *Ringmaster II* before the designers make the final changes."

"Wow!" Henry said. "We'd get to see it way ahead of everybody else."

"I'm told there's one condition before we go over there," Grandfather went on. "John's nephew told him that before trying the new game, it's important to become a Ringmaster on the first game. Now I hope one of you will tell me what a Ringmaster is."

Benny jumped up and down. "That's what we turn into if we find the magic ring. Soo Lee and I are almost Ringmasters."

Grandfather shuffled a deck of playing

cards. "Well, I'll leave magic rings and computer games to you children. I use the computer for reports often enough. But when it comes to games, I prefer a simple game of solitaire. I want to become a Solitaire Master!"

The children returned to their computer. They started up *Ringmaster* where they had left it.

"We're getting close," Jessie said when the sound and pictures came on. "The two youngest children and their dog, Tracker, are right near that waterfall."

Benny put his hand on the mouse. "First the boy and girl have to finish eating. I wonder if there's a biscuit in their packs for Tracker."

Benny clicked the mouse. The computer boy poured himself a drink from a container. Just as he lifted the cup to his lips, Soo Lee cried out, "Look, Benny! There's green steam coming out of the drink. Maybe something bad is in it."

Benny hit a key on the keyboard and read aloud the message that popped up:

"Should this liquid cross your lip,
Never shall you drink another sip.
Yet set aside at least a drop,
Every enemy shall you stop."

"Phew!" he said. "You warned me just in time, Soo Lee, or else the game would be over for me."

He hit another key and continued with the game.

The smoking poison liquid dripped from the cup. It landed on the ground, sizzled, and a hole opened up large enough to explore. Benny and Soo Lee took turns guiding the two computer children through the underground passageway. At the other end they found a spooky forest. One strange tree had branches like arms and twigs like fingers.

"Eeee!" the Aldens screamed when the tree branches turned into a twisted hand.

The hand reached out for the boy and girl. Even Tracker, their dog, wasn't safe.

Violet took over the mouse and clicked on another tree covered with apples.

"Look, the apples have smiley faces!" Soo Lee said. "This must be a good tree."

Several clicks later, Violet had the computer children safely resting in the branches of the magic apple tree.

Henry and Jessie then took turns using the mouse to guide the children through dangerous adventures until all the computer children and their dog were found and brought together.

"All together. Just like us," Soo Lee said.

The computer children stood at the bottom of a hill that arose from a valley.

"Doesn't that hill look odd?" Jessie asked. "It's all covered with vines."

Soo Lee remembered the tree with the finger branches. "Ooo. Be careful."

Jessie had an idea. She tipped the container of poison liquid to drop a little on the vines. Instantly the vines shriveled up. "Look! There's an old house underneath the vines!" she cried, pleased with her decision.

Benny clicked the claw-shaped door knocker, the door creaked open, and the computer children, along with Tracker, stepped into a cavelike room.

On-screen, the Aldens saw a large gold bell with a rim of jewels at the bottom.

"What do the words on the bell say, Jessie?" Soo Lee asked.

Jessie read them aloud:

"Behold, to find the ring you seek,
Within your treasures you must peek.
Present yourselves all alone,
Not one minute do postpone.
Make your offerings to the bell,
Give every wish and every spell."

Benny tugged at Jessie's elbow. "What should we do?"

Jessie thought for a second. "I have a feeling the characters must give up all the magic in their packs before they can find the ring."

Benny wasn't so sure about this. "We can't! What if we need some of the spells and things?"

Jessie put her arm around Benny. "At the end of stories and games like *Ringmaster*, the characters sometimes have to go through the hardest part of their quest all by themselves, with no magic to help them."

Each of the children took a turn clicking on the backpacks of the on-screen children.

When the last pack was empty, another pop-up message appeared. This time Violet read it:

> "*Behold, you stand before the bell*
> *Empty-handed, without a spell.*
> *Think hard and think faster,*
> *Ring the bell to become a Ringmaster.*"

Violet stared at the jeweled bell on the screen. She clicked on it, but nothing happened. " 'Ring the bell,' " she said. "I wonder what that really means." She stared some more. "Wait! Let me try one more

thing." With that, she guided the mouse to place all the children on-screen in a circle around the jeweled rim of the bell. Suddenly the bell separated, leaving a beautiful jeweled ring floating by itself in the air.

"You made a ring around the bell, Violet," Henry said. "That's what the message meant. Look, the Magician is coming on-screen."

In his royal blue robes, the Magician walked over to the ring and picked it up. "I pronounce you Ringmasters!" his voice rang out through the computer speaker. "You have found the ring. Game over."

The Aldens jumped up and down.

"We won the game!" Benny yelled. "Now we're real Ringmasters. Hooray!"

CHAPTER 2

A New Quest

The next afternoon, the Aldens headed out for their appointment at the QuestMaster Company, just outside Greenfield.

"I've never driven a car full of magic Ringmasters around before," Grandfather said. "And here's the place where they make the magic," he added when he turned into the QuestMaster parking lot.

Benny stared at the ordinary brick building up ahead. "That? It sure doesn't look like much."

Indeed, there wasn't a cave or a castle or a haunted house in sight. The small sign in front of the large brick building said QUESTMASTER in plain letters — nothing like the red-and-yellow flame letters on the *Ringmaster* game box.

"Don't be too disappointed," Mr. Alden said when he parked the car. "My friend John Romer said his nephew, Charles, designed the building for hard work and hard play, too. There's a playing field in back, a basketball court, video games, pool tables, and the like. Some of the employees here even bring their dogs to work."

"You mean we could have brought Watch?" Jessie asked.

Grandfather nodded. "Perhaps — though I'm not sure Watch is ready to sit in front of a computer just yet."

"Just under the computer," Benny said.

The children laughed at the thought of Watch going to a big office. Yet, just outside the QuestMaster building, the Aldens noticed several dogs playing in a fenced dog run. Next to that, they saw several people playing basketball outside.

Henry and Jessie looked at each other.

"Wouldn't it be fun to work in a place where you could bring your dog and play basketball at lunch?" Jessie asked.

A tall young man with sandy hair, freckles, and blue eyes spotted the Aldens on the sidelines. He waved them over, then tossed the ball to Jessie. Soon all the Aldens, except for Grandfather, had joined the basketball game. Many of the players were wearing bright red *Ringmaster* shirts.

"This is fun," Benny said to Henry a few minutes later. "Only that lady over there doesn't pass the ball."

Henry nodded. He, too, had noticed that the young woman with the ponytail grabbed the ball a lot and didn't pass it much. She was a pretty good player, though, and made lots of baskets.

Finally the game was over.

"Hi, Aldens," the young man said, holding out his hand to Mr. Alden, then to the

children. "I've been expecting you. I'm Charles David Romer, but around here everybody calls me C.D. That was pretty good playing."

The Aldens looked surprised. This young man was the founder of QuestMaster? Although he was in his midtwenties, he didn't look much older than Henry.

"I'm the boss around here," C.D. said when he realized the Aldens still didn't quite know who he was.

"You don't look bossy," Benny blurted out.

This made the Aldens laugh and feel right at home.

Mr. Alden introduced the children by name.

"Hi," C.D. said as he went around shaking each of the Aldens' hands. "Here comes one of our new designers. This dynamo hoop star is Jane Driver. Jane just started work here last month. Jane, meet the Aldens. They're going to be testing out some of the new *Ringmaster II* stuff we've been working on."

The young woman didn't seem interested in the Aldens. "I have to get back to work, C.D.," she said before rushing indoors.

"Jane would spend all her time on game design if I let her. But I don't let her," C.D. said. "In a company like QuestMaster, we all share ideas. So we play a lot of group games to encourage everyone to work together. Jane's not used to our way of working yet."

"We are!" Benny announced. "We work together while we're having fun. That's how we got to be Ringmasters."

C.D. gave Benny a high five. "Way to go, Benny! Uncle John was right to send you over to help us out," C.D. told the Aldens as he led them inside the building to a small room.

He pulled out a box of red *Ringmaster* T-shirts and gave one to each of the children. "After you try these on, meet me in the design studio," C.D. said to the children. "It's down that hall and through the door. See you later, Mr. Alden. I'll have the computer and your grandchildren all ready to go at five o'clock. Meet us at our loading dock."

After their grandfather left, the children walked down the hall and opened a door. They were surprised to find themselves in a huge room.

"This room is almost as big as the school gym," Jessie said. "I've never seen so many computers in one place, either. Plus two pool tables. What a funny place QuestMaster is. I can't tell if it's a place to work or a place to play."

All along the walls, a dozen or so people were working in front of large-screen computers. All the screens showed the same thing — a mean-looking dragon about to pounce on Tracker, the little game dog from *Ringmaster I.*

"Look at that!" Henry said. He was thrilled to get a sneak peek at his favorite game.

C.D. spotted the Aldens across the studio. "Hey, everybody. It's okay to leave your work on-screen," he told all the designers. "Meet the Aldens. They're here to help us test out our new game."

C.D. led the children to the fanciest computer they had ever seen. "Come meet Morka, our dragon character," he said. "Our designers are trying to decide what kind of dragon we want Morka to be. Right now we've made him a scary dragon. He's after Tracker, one of our favorite characters."

A real dog, not a computer dog, came out from under one of the nearby desks. He was scruffy, with rough gray fur. He wagged his tail and sniffed at the Aldens.

"He smells our dog, Watch, on our clothes," Jessie told C.D.

"He's the original Tracker," C.D. explained, "and our QuestMaster mascot, too. I found him wandering near our old offices a couple of years ago. So I modeled our computer dog after him."

"Our dog, Watch, is a good tracker," Benny said. "He tracked us when we lived in the woods."

C.D. scratched Tracker's head before the dog went back to his nap spot under the desk. "Sometimes people find dogs, and sometimes dogs find people. Bring Watch in sometime. Anyway, how do you like the look of this dragon so far? Too scary?"

"No way!" Benny answered.

C.D. sat down in front of his computer again. He fiddled with some controls and did some amazing art tricks on-screen. "How about this?" he asked after he added a pair of pink wings to the dragon.

"Now he's a nice dragon," Soo Lee said.

C.D. offered each of the Aldens a turn at the computer. They turned Morka into a fish-faced dragon, then a cat-faced dragon, then back to a scary dragon again.

"Maybe Morka can be a dragon that changes all the time," Violet suggested, "depending on what's happening in the game."

C.D. gave Violet a big smile. "Great idea! We'll be trying a lot of new things on *Ringmaster III* after this game is sent out to the stores. Jane Driver came up with something no other game has — it's top secret right now."

The next thing everyone heard was a crash nearby.

"What on earth was that?" C.D. asked.

C.D. walked over to the next workstation. A tall, dark-haired man was picking up papers, photos, and computer disks that had fallen to the floor.

"Is everything okay, Ned?" C.D. asked. "That was quite a racket."

The man's face was angry-looking. "Talk about racket! I'll tell you what's a racket — a pack of kids running around an office."

This didn't much bother C.D. "Hold your horses, Ned. You know this place isn't a library."

"It's not a playground, either," Ned said. "A man can't get a minute's quiet here."

C.D. chuckled. "Now, Ned. You know QuestMaster is part playground, part office. After all, what are we designing here? Games for kids. Now take a break, okay? You've been working too hard. Come meet the Aldens. According to their grandfather, they've got a reputation for solving problems and mysteries. Kids, meet one of our head designers, Ned Porter. He's responsible for a lot of great ideas in *Ringmaster I* and *II*."

Ned Porter brushed right by the Aldens.

"Should we go home?" Jessie asked.

C.D. laughed. "No way! Ned's been kind of grumpy lately. I wish I knew what was bothering him. Maybe he's just been working too hard. Now let's go back to my computer so you can try out *Ringmaster II*. That's why I brought you here."

When it was nearly five o'clock, the children had been exploring *Ringmaster II* for a few hours.

"So what do you think of our new game so far?" C.D. asked.

"Amazing," Henry said. "There are a lot of new features and characters."

C.D. beamed. "Glad you like it. Wait until next year when you get a look at *Ring-*

master III. We're experimenting right now with that new feature Jane Driver came up with."

The children held their breath. Maybe this time C.D. would let them in on the big secret.

"Sorry, guys," C.D. told them. "I can't tell you what it is. If Jane and I work out all the bugs, *Ringmaster III* is going to bring computer games to a whole new level, just you wait."

Benny rocked back and forth on his sneakers. "I can't wait."

C.D. smiled at the Aldens. "One thing you don't have to wait for is that computer I promised you. Follow me. Your grandfather is probably waiting at our loading dock now."

"This looks like a computer store," Jessie said when C.D. led the children to a storage room packed with computers.

"These are practically brand-new," C.D. explained. "We replaced them because all the artwork we've been doing on *Ringmaster II* soaks up a lot more power." He walked up and down the room. "Now, where's the one I set aside for you?"

With the Aldens trailing behind, C.D. turned down another aisle. When he did, he nearly bumped into Jane Driver.

"Whoa, Jane!" C.D. said. "What are you doing in here?"

Jane looked flustered when the Aldens crowded around her. "The sound card on my new computer isn't working. I was going to remove the one from my old machine."

C.D. looked puzzled. "Sorry, Jane. You really can't do that. Just ask Ned to help you figure out how to use the new card. I want all these computers I'm donating to the high school to go out fully equipped. Your old one is going to the Aldens. They'll need the sound card for testing out parts of *Ringmaster II*."

Jane's face grew red. "But . . ."

C.D. grew a bit impatient. "Look, Jane, please go find Andy Porter now. I need him to carry the monitor out to Mr. Alden's car, and that's that."

Jane seemed frozen in place.

"The sound card should stay in this machine," C.D. repeated. "Now please find Andy for us."

A long time seemed to pass before Jane moved. When she finally left, she pushed the swinging doors so hard they swung back and forth several times before coming to a stop.

CHAPTER 3

Eavesdropping

When the Aldens arrived at the loading dock, Grandfather was already there. He opened his car trunk so C.D. and Henry could put the computer and keyboard inside.

Jessie found the Aldens' old picnic blanket and wrapped it around the equipment. "That'll keep everything from bumping around back here," she told Grandfather. "We can put the monitor on the other side so it doesn't slip and slide."

C.D. checked his watch. "Where is that

monitor, anyway? Andy Porter should have been here by now. I hope Jane gave him my message. Why don't you kids run back to the storage area and look around for Andy. Maybe he needs some help."

"Don't you mean *Ned* Porter?" asked Benny.

"Andy is Ned's son. They're both computer whizzes, and they both work here," said C.D.

The Aldens headed inside. As they got closer to the computer storage room, they overheard two people arguing.

"Dad! You can't let that happen. It's not fair," one person said.

"Stay out of it," a second person answered. "I'll take care of things."

Jessie signaled to Henry to turn around. The children tiptoed out, wondering what the argument was about.

"Any luck?" C.D. asked when the Aldens reappeared without Andy. "Oh, there he is, right behind you."

The children whirled around. Standing

behind them was a teenage boy about Henry's age. Andy looked very much like his father, dark-haired, tall, and serious. On a hand truck in front of him was a large computer monitor box.

"Thanks for getting our monitor," Henry told Andy. "I'm Henry. These are my sisters, Jessie and Violet, my brother, Benny, and our cousin, Soo Lee."

Andy smiled shyly. Without a word, he rolled the hand truck and the monitor down the ramp where C.D. and Mr. Alden were standing.

"What took so long, Andy?" C.D. asked.

The boy didn't answer right away. "I . . . uh . . . couldn't find an empty box right away. Sorry."

C.D. smiled at the boy. "Meet Mr. Alden."

"Glad to meet you, young man," Mr. Alden said. "Charles has told me what a valuable worker you are. I'm sure my grandchildren can learn a lot from you."

The Aldens couldn't tell if Andy thought

this was a compliment or not. He seemed confused at being surrounded by so many strangers. "Is it true that your grandchildren are good at solving mysteries?" he asked quietly. "My father told me C.D. said they were."

"They have solved more than a few," Grandfather said, "but I think they've moved on to figuring out computer games."

C.D. grinned at Grandfather in reply and helped Andy load the computer box into the trunk. "Andy works part-time keeping track of our equipment," C.D. began. "But he gets as much done as many of my full-time workers. Plus he's an ace on computers, to boot."

When Benny heard this, he laughed. "I know how to boot the computer. That means starting it up."

C.D. gave Benny a friendly shoulder punch. "Good for you. That's exactly what booting up means. Well, now you Aldens have some pretty up-to-date equipment. You can boot up parts of *Ringmaster II* and get onto our network as well. Just let me know by e-mail if you find anything strange."

"The Aldens are going to be on the QuestMaster network?" Andy asked.

C.D. nodded. "Some parts of it, like e-mail. They'll be looking for bugs and testing out some of the new things we're introducing in *Ringmaster II*."

"But — but I thought everything was a secret," Andy said, looking confused again.

C.D. laughed. "Not much longer, Andy. We just have to work out those bugs. And I need some real live children to run through the game before we do the final version."

Andy's face grew red. "I thought that's why you hired me."

C.D. gave Andy an encouraging smile. "It is, but you already know the game so well. Plus I need you to keep the machines running tip-top. But we need younger kids, too. Violet, Benny, and Soo Lee are just the right ages to try out all the levels of the game and make sure the clues are easy to follow."

Benny just had to speak up when he heard this. "Soo Lee and I figure out *hard* clues, too, not just easy ones."

"I told Benny not to let the boy in the game drink the juice," Soo Lee added. "It was poison."

Everyone but Andy Porter laughed.

C.D. stared at Andy for a few seconds. "I'm counting on you to get the Aldens' computer set up for them. Now let's lift this monitor into Mr. Alden's car."

Andy did as he was told. He even did something he wasn't told. While C.D. chatted with Mr. Alden and the children after they got into the car, Benny watched Andy from the backseat. After a few minutes, he whispered to Soo Lee, "Let's go see what Andy's doing." Quietly they got out of the car.

When Soo Lee and Benny crept up behind Andy, he was unwrapping the computer. He took out a small flashlight and looked at the back.

Benny was curious about what Andy was up to. "Whatcha doing?"

Andy jumped back, nearly bumping his head on the station wagon's rear door. He didn't answer Benny or Soo Lee right away.

"How come you're doing that? Is something wrong with the computer?"

"I needed to check something," Andy whispered. "It's easier for me to concentrate if I'm by myself. I'm almost done, so you can get back in the car."

Benny and Soo Lee quietly returned to the car and buckled themselves in.

Mr. Alden started the car. He checked the rearview mirror. "I guess Andy is all done with whatever he was doing."

"He was just packing up," C.D. told Mr. Alden as he stepped away from the driver's window.

"He had a teeny flashlight — " Soo Lee piped up from the backseat.

"And — and . . ." Benny interrupted. "And he was looking at the back of the computer and everything."

"Hmm," C.D. said before going around to the back of Mr. Alden's car. "Andy, any problems with this computer?"

The children turned around. They saw Andy put his hands in his pockets. He didn't quite look at C.D. "Uh . . . no. It's just that . . . well, since Jane Driver only used this computer a short time, I thought we . . . uh . . . we were keeping it. She took it home last week, so I didn't get a chance to check it with the others."

This didn't bother C.D. a bit. "No problem. I'll send you around to the Aldens' if they need help. Mind you, Mr. Alden says Henry and Jessie can probably handle any difficulties."

Andy suddenly seemed to remember something. "I'll help the Aldens set up this one tomorrow."

The children had other ideas.

"Jessie and I like fooling with computers, too," Henry told Andy out the car window. "We probably won't need you to come over. We should be okay. But thanks for the offer."

"Yeah, well, our computer software and games aren't as easy to set up as they look," Andy said. "I'll come over to help you."

"You don't know my grandchildren, Andy," Mr. Alden said. "They'll stay up all night trying to solve a problem before they'll call for help. But you're welcome to come by our place anytime just for fun. By the way, how are you at checkers?"

Andy Porter looked confused by all these Aldens and their questions, but he smiled anyway. "I have the highest score at Quest-Master on computer checkers."

Mr. Alden shook his head. "Is there anyone left who still likes a nice quiet game of old-fashioned checkers?"

"I do, Grandfather," Violet answered. "Let's have a game when we get home."

At those words, Mr. Alden pulled away from the loading dock. "So long, C.D. So long, Andy."

C.D. waved, but Andy Porter had already disappeared into the building.

"Maybe Andy wanted the computer C.D. gave us for himself," Henry said.

"Only now we have it," Benny added. "Because we're the Ringmasters."

CHAPTER 4

Whispers at Breakfast

Mr. Alden had to wait for his game of checkers. The children spent the whole evening getting their new computer up and running.

The next morning, they went straight to the computer before breakfast.

"Looks like another day of playing solitaire, not checkers," Grandfather said when the children disappeared into the den. He was smiling, though. Mr. Alden always enjoyed watching his grandchildren's excitement over a new project.

In no time Jessie had *Ringmaster I* up and running just to see how fast it worked on the new computer. "Wow, this is super-fast. We could have become Ringmasters sooner on this new one."

Henry and Jessie tested out the Quest-Master network next.

"Hey, we've got mail," Jessie said when she heard the computer beep. "It's from Andy. He must have sent this overnight." She clicked open the e-mail and read it aloud to the other children:

"I'll be over in the morning to set up all the software and games you need."

Soo Lee tugged at Henry's elbow. "Andy is too late, right, Henry? You and Jessie did it all by yourselves."

Henry smiled at Soo Lee. "Not by ourselves. Everybody helped."

The next thing the children heard was Watch barking. Benny scooted after Watch. "Somebody's at the door."

Mrs. McGregor was already there, talking to someone. "I'll go check with the children. Were they expecting you?"

"Hi, Andy," Benny said when he saw Andy Porter standing in the doorway.

"Hi, Benny. Did you get my e-mail?" Andy asked. "I came over to get everything going like C.D. asked me to."

By this time Soo Lee had followed Benny out to the hallway. "My cousins know everything. They put *Ringmaster I* and *II* on the computer. Henry's trying *Ringmaster II* now. It's very hard but not too hard for Henry."

"What's the matter?" Benny asked when he noticed that Andy looked upset.

"I wish they hadn't installed the game without me," Andy said. "They could have made a lot of mistakes."

"Henry and Jessie hardly ever make mistakes," Benny said. "Want to see?"

Benny and Soo Lee led Andy into the den. Henry and Jessie were glued to the computer. Up on the screen, Morka the dragon was breathing flames at the on-screen children.

"You won't let the boy and girl get burned, right?" Soo Lee asked Henry.

Henry kept his hand on one of the keys and his eyes on the screen. "Don't worry about that, Soo Lee. Now, just watch."

Watch thumped his tail under the desk.

"No, silly," Soo Lee said to Watch. "Henry means watch the screen."

With one click, Henry sent a storm cloud chasing after Morka. Rain poured from the cloud onto Morka's flaming breath. The dragon melted into a big green puddle. The boy and girl and Tracker were safe!

"Good for you, Henry," Jessie said. When she turned around, she was surprised to see Andy standing there. "Andy! We read your e-mail. I guess you didn't get our answer in time. We could have saved you a trip. As you can see, we got the new computer and everything going — even the QuestMaster programs, the same ones you use at work."

Andy was so busy looking over Jessie's shoulder, he didn't seem to hear what she said. "Well, I . . . uh . . . needed to come over anyway. We just made some adjustments on the game, and I came over to add a couple of new features to *Ringmaster II*. It'll just take me a minute to reprogram the changes."

Jessie and Henry looked at each other. They were proud that they had set up the computer all by themselves. They didn't know quite what to do now that Andy was here.

"C.D. said to come over, remember?" Andy said.

Jessie moved off her chair, and Andy took her place.

Henry didn't move.

Andy wriggled in the chair. "Know what? It's hard for me to work when people are watching. When I'm *done*, though, I bet you'll want to check out everything again."

"But Grandfather says that's how we learn, by watching," Benny said.

Andy's ears got nearly as red as his *Ringmaster* T-shirt.

"It's okay, Andy," Henry said finally. "We'll go have breakfast while you're fixing things."

"Mrs. McGregor is fixing things, too,"

Jessie said to cheer everyone up, including Andy. "She made waffles. Let's get some in the kitchen. When you're done with the computer, Andy, take a left down the hallway. Just follow the waffle smell to find the kitchen."

She smiled at Andy, but he didn't even look up from the computer.

At breakfast Mrs. McGregor set down an extra plate. "Where's your friend?"

"Working on the computer," Henry whispered. "We invited him for breakfast, but he didn't answer."

Benny looked up at Mrs. McGregor. "If he doesn't eat his waffles, may I have seconds?"

Mrs. McGregor smiled. "First have firsts, Benny. Andy might get hungry in a while."

Jessie stared at the maple syrup pitcher without picking it up. "Doesn't it seem strange that Andy already had a new *Ringmaster II* section to add, when they are still having problems with the game?" she said in a whisper. "C.D. never mentioned that yesterday afternoon."

Henry turned to look down the hallway. "I was thinking the same thing," he whispered back.

Jessie remembered something. "Didn't you say you saw Andy unwrap the computer in the trunk and check it with a flashlight?" she asked the younger children.

Benny and Soo Lee nodded.

Violet put down her fork. She dabbed the corners of her mouth with her napkin. "Maybe Andy thought C.D. was going to give *him* the computer that he gave to us instead. After all, it's supposed to be pretty new."

Henry put down his glass of milk. "Good guess, Violet," he said in a loud whisper. "Or else Jane wanted to keep that computer for home or something. That might explain why neither of them is too friendly with us."

"Or else there's something about the computer C.D. gave us that's different from the others," Jessie noted. "First Jane Driver seemed upset that we had it, now Andy is."

Violet disagreed. "I think Andy just wants

to help us out." She picked up Andy's plate and a glass of milk. "I know we're not supposed to eat near the computer, but may I bring these to Andy?" Violet asked Mrs. McGregor. "Maybe he forgot to eat, since he came over here to help us out."

Mrs. McGregor nodded. "Of course. Here's one more waffle for him — a hot one, nice and crisp."

Violet walked slowly down the hallway to the den.

"Andy?" she called as she came into the den.

But there was no Andy to answer her or to take the food she had brought him. The den was silent except for the *Ringmaster II* music playing quietly from the computer speakers.

Now that the Aldens had their computer back to themselves, they decided to finish the game of *Ringmaster II* they had started.

"Did you wash your hands, you two?" Jessie asked Benny and Soo Lee after breakfast. "No sticky fingers on the keyboard."

"I don't know why Andy went without saying good-bye," Henry said. "He's a hard one to figure out, that's for sure."

Jessie pulled her chair up to the computer. "I wonder if that was Andy and his father we overheard arguing at the warehouse yesterday."

"I think so but I couldn't tell for sure," Henry answered. "They both sounded pretty upset. For such a great place, QuestMaster has a few grumpy people working there. And a mystery, too: Problems keep coming up with *Ringmaster II.*"

Henry restarted *Ringmaster II*. The screen the children had been playing on before breakfast came up. But it looked as if there was something new in the game.

"Are my eyes fooling me?" Henry asked the other children. "When we were on this screen before, the pictures were a little different. Maybe this is one of the bugs C.D. was talking about. I didn't notice that sign — the one over the castle door. It says, '*The Brass Horn.*' "

"That's a funny name for a castle," Jessie said.

Benny didn't think so at all. "That's the name of our good lunch place in Greenfield, the one that's almost like a castle inside. Maybe it's a clue that we should go there for lunch! Remember, when we gave the troll food on the computer, Mrs. McGregor brought us food, too?"

Jessie laughed. "I don't think the computer can hear your stomach talking, Benny!"

Violet stared at the on-screen castle. "What if Benny's right? Isn't it a little funny that the name of the castle is the same name as a restaurant in Greenfield? Look at the old wooden marker on the tree. It says, 'Forest Lane.' "

Benny leaned against Henry and glued his nose to the screen. "Hey, the Brass Horn Restaurant is on Forest Lane! And the clock on the castle tower says twelve o'clock, right, Jessie? That's lunchtime."

Jessie and Henry looked at each other.

Were Benny and Violet on to something?

Jessie spoke first. "It would be pretty weird if a clue in a computer game was pointing to something *outside of the computer game*, to something in *real* life."

"Probably a coincidence," Henry finally decided.

Benny patted his stomach. "Being hungry isn't a coincidence. It happens every day. If we walked all the way to the Brass Horn, I think I would be hungry by the time we got there."

All the other children laughed.

"All right. I give in," Henry said. "I'll ask Grandfather and Mrs. McGregor if we can go there for lunch. Right now I want to explore this game some more."

Henry was soon lost in *Ringmaster II* again. He began to click his way through the new game. Then he stopped.

"What's the matter?" Soo Lee asked when she saw Henry staring hard at the screen. "Who's that scary lady hiding in the castle?"

Henry clicked on a two-headed, green-faced woman. " 'Nadje,' " Henry read on the screen when the name popped up in a little box. When Henry clicked again, another pop-up box appeared over the character's head:

Her two faces do you see,
One for them and one for thee.
Follow her footsteps wherever she goes,
But be careful to stay in the shadows.

"Wow, this is getting exciting!" Henry said. "I guess we're supposed to keep an eye on Nadje while we look for the ring. She must be dangerous."

"I don't remember seeing her character when we tried out *Ringmaster II* before. Don't you think that's strange?" Jessie asked Henry. "Check the character list."

Henry slid the computer mouse over to Jessie. She pulled down a list of characters. He moved the arrow keys up and down the screen. "There's no Nadje listed. Maybe the designers just added her to the game but haven't had time to put her name on the list yet. I'm going to exit the game and e-mail C.D. about Nadje."

When Henry tried to send his e-mail, a warning box came on. He read it aloud for the other children.

"We are unable to send or receive e-mail at this time. Please do not use the QuestMaster network until further notice. Someone from the office will check your computer shortly. Please note that you should attend the meeting scheduled this afternoon at one o'clock in the Quest-Master studio."

Henry shut down the QuestMaster network. "I wonder if C.D. has two screen names. That message was signed with the name EyeSpy. I'd better do what it says. I don't want to cause a computer crash or anything."

"Is there a crash?" Soo Lee asked her cousin. "Are you going to call the police?"

Henry patted Soo Lee's hand. "A computer crash isn't like a car crash. It's some kind of problem that needs to be fixed inside the program or the computer."

Benny looked as if someone had taken his favorite toy away. "But we didn't really get much chance to try the new game. Is the computer really broken?"

Jessie stood behind Henry at the keyboard. "No problem, Benny. The message just said not to use the network. We can open *Ringmaster II* separately. Why don't you give it a try, Violet?"

Violet took Henry's place in front of the computer. Benny and Soo Lee shared the chair next to her.

"I think I'll follow what the two-headed lady does," Violet said. "Don't worry, Soo Lee. There are some special spells in the little kids' saddlebags on their horse. Look who's in the other saddlebag."

Soo Lee smiled at the screen. "Tracker!"

When Violet clicked on a spell in the saddlebags, the horse the two children were riding stopped at the castle gate.

"Uh-oh," Soo Lee said. "The lady with two heads pulled up the drawbridge. How will you get the horse over the wall?"

The children carried on with the game. Again and again they were stopped by the two-headed Nadje.

"She keeps stopping us," Soo Lee complained.

"If we can't get to the end of *Ringmaster II*, we won't be any help to C.D.," added Benny.

"Maybe we should use all of our magic spells to get rid of her," Violet suggested.

Jessie looked on thoughtfully as Violet moved the pointer across the screen. "It might take more than magic," she said softly.

CHAPTER 5

A Lunchtime Mystery

Grandfather's grandfather clock chimed the half hour at eleven-thirty.

"Can we go to lunch now?" Benny asked. "I like this new game, but now I'm hungry. Those waffles were a long time ago."

"Three whole hours," Jessie said, laughing. She jiggled Watch's red leash, which was hanging in the hallway. "All right, Watch, you can come, too."

Watch licked Jessie's hand as if he understood everything she said.

The children said good-bye to Grandfather and Mrs. McGregor, who were going out grocery shopping.

Walking to the Brass Horn Restaurant took a long time. Watch liked to stop at every tree and bark at every squirrel that he saw. He even barked at a green car that drove down the Aldens' street twice.

"I wonder what the meeting at Quest-Master is about this afternoon," Jessie said. "It came up so suddenly."

Henry walked ahead of the other children. He was eager to find out why C.D. wanted everyone at the studio. "I sure hope it's to tell us about Jane's secret idea." Henry reached into his back pocket and stopped.

"What's the matter, Henry?" Soo Lee asked.

Henry smacked his forehead. "I forgot my wallet on the front hall table. The money Grandfather gave us for our lunch is in it."

Soo Lee dug into her pocket. "I have seven cents."

Benny turned his jeans pockets inside out. "I have a quarter."

The older children smiled.

"I think we'll need Henry's wallet," Jessie said.

As soon as the Aldens turned onto their street, Watch jerked ahead, with Violet at his heels. "Slow down, Watch!" she said. "What's the matter?"

Watch barked and pulled Violet toward the house.

Jessie noticed a green car parked in the driveway. "There's a man ringing the doorbell. I wonder if Grandfather was expecting someone. That's the car that I saw going past us before." She spoke to Watch in a soothing voice. "It's okay, Watch."

But seeing a strange man on the Alden porch was not okay with Watch. He always barked when someone new came to the door.

The man heard the barking and turned around.

"It's Ned Porter!" Jessie cried, waving to

get his attention. "Hi, Ned. Did you come over to fix our computer?"

Ned Porter didn't answer. Instead he went down the porch steps quickly, got in his car, and drove away.

"Why didn't he wait for us?" Benny wanted to know.

No one had the answer to that. The children let themselves inside the house. Henry found his wallet where he'd left it.

"Is there enough for hamburgers?" Benny asked Henry.

"As many as you want," Henry answered.

The Aldens were plenty hungry after their long walk to the Brass Horn Restaurant.

"See?" Benny said to everyone. "The computer was right. It's twelve o'clock, and we're at the Brass Horn on Forest Lane. And . . . what else?"

"And you're hungry!" Jessie tickled Benny's side.

The Brass Horn was a nice old restaurant in Greenfield where Grandfather often brought the children. He told them it was very much like restaurants he had visited in England. Inside, there was a stone fireplace, old wooden beams, and paintings of knights and castles and horses. There was even a brass hunting horn over the doorway. In the summer, customers could eat outside at the big old wooden tables. Everyone drank from pewter mugs and ate from pewter plates, just as in olden times.

Jessie tied Watch's leash to a big shady tree just beyond the patio. "Be a good boy, Watch. We'll be right over there, eating outside."

"Hello, Aldens," the hostess said when she saw the children. "Where's your grandfather today?"

"Grandfather let us come here all by ourselves," Benny answered. "And we even brought Watch. Jessie tied his leash to your big tree."

The hostess smiled at the children. "I've got the perfect table for you, then, right next to that tree. You can watch Watch."

The children liked the large menus,

which were written in old-fashioned letters.

Benny already knew what he wanted, so he looked around at the other people in the restaurant over the top of his menu. That's when he happened to notice a familiar face. "Don't look now," he whispered from behind his menu. "But that lady from Quest-Master, Jane Driver, is over there."

The other children buried their noses behind their menus. One by one they took a peek across the patio.

"You're right, Benny!" Henry whispered. "I wonder who those two men are, sitting with her."

Jessie tried not to stare. "They have papers spread out over their table. They don't look like anybody we've met at Quest-Master. Should we go over there and say hi?"

Violet turned around slowly to catch a peek, too. "One of them just got up to use the phone."

Just then the children heard Watch bark.

"Oh, no," Jessie said. "What could Watch be barking about? He's always so quiet and polite when we take him out. He only barks near home."

Jessie went over to scold Watch, then returned to the table. "You'll never guess who's over there behind Jane's table. Ned! That's who Watch was barking at."

"This is getting interesting," Henry said. "Ned is standing right behind Jane, as if he's trying to hear what's going on. Why doesn't he just let her know he's there?"

After the waiter took the Aldens' orders, he took their menus away. They couldn't hide anymore.

"It doesn't matter," Violet said. "Jane and Ned can't see us from where they are. And the two men with Jane wouldn't recognize us anyway."

"Nothing is happening over there," Benny said a while later. "Except that Jane and Ned are in the same restaurant but not together. What could be wrong with that?"

"Nothing," Henry agreed, "but I have a funny feeling something is going on with Jane and Ned. I wonder what it is. Let's see what they have to say at the meeting later."

CHAPTER 6

Wrong Information

Watch began sniffing as soon as the Aldens and Soo Lee arrived at Quest-Master. A security guard recognized them from their earlier visit and let them in. Watch could tell right away that dogs were welcome there.

Tracker came out from hiding under C.D.'s computer desk.

"Hi, Tracker," Jessie said. "Meet Watch. Watch, meet Tracker." She turned to the other children. "Well, the dogs are here, but where are the people?"

The design studio was deserted. Not even C.D. seemed to be around. Tracker and Watch soon began chasing each other around the empty office.

"This place is going to the dogs," Henry joked. He checked his watch. "I wonder if we got the time wrong."

"Hello! Hello!" Jessie shouted, but no one answered back.

Where was everyone? Finally the children heard footsteps.

"Hey, Aldens," C.D. said when he came into the studio. "What brings you here?"

The children didn't speak at first. They just stared at one another in confusion.

"Isn't there a meeting at one o'clock?" Henry asked. "We got an e-mail this morning saying to come here. Are you EyeSpy? I thought maybe you were using a funny screen name."

C.D. laughed. "It's not me. I have a feeling someone was playing a prank on you. Sorry about that. Sometimes people on my staff get bored and start sending funny e-mails. There's no meeting scheduled."

Jessie wondered about this. "But the message wasn't funny. It said to come to a meeting today. It also said not to use the network and that somebody would come to fix it."

C.D. looked confused now. "We haven't had any network problem that I know of. We're still looking for bugs in *Ringmaster II*. And I've been having problems with that new feature for *Ringmaster III* that Jane created. Now she's telling me she can't get it to work anymore. She went off to Hampstead this morning for a special computer chip she heard about that might get her idea working again."

"Does it have anything to do with *Ringmaster II*?" Benny asked. "There's a two-headed character named Nadje."

"Nadje?" C.D. asked. "Are you sure of the name? I've never heard of any two-headed character. Sounds interesting. When did you discover this character?"

"This morning," Henry said. "That's the weird thing. When we played the *Ringmaster II* software here the other day and then

at home, we didn't see any Nadje character."

"Or any sign on the castle that said 'The
Brass Horn,' either," Violet added. "That's
the same name as the restaurant in Greenfield where we just saw — "

Jessie gently poked Violet. She didn't feel
right about telling C.D. that they had spied
Jane Driver in the restaurant when C.D.
thought she was in Hampstead.

C.D. booted up the nearest computer,
which happened to be Ned's. "Okay, Aldens, see if you can bring up this Nadje
character somewhere in this game."

Henry and Jessie tried to remember what
keys they had hit when they discovered
Nadje. But every time they got to the on-
screen castle, only the evil Wumps appeared.

"Are you sure you're doing it right?"
C.D. asked. "I don't see this Nadje character. And there's no sign over the castle, either."

"Maybe we accidentally hit some wrong
keys," Jessie said. "That might have brought

up parts of the game someone left in by mistake when they were designing it," Jessie said.

Before they could say anything to C.D., though, he had turned off the game, for something else on Ned's screen caught his attention. "What on earth . . ." he murmured. He opened up a file marked "Head Shots," and suddenly several rows of color photographs appeared on the screen.

"Wow!" said Henry.

"Ned shouldn't have these," said C.D. in a serious tone.

"Is it the secret?" asked Soo Lee.

"They look like pictures of people who work at QuestMaster," Jessie said. "And some of their dogs. I'm confused. Why shouldn't Ned have them?"

C.D. didn't answer right away. When he did, he spoke very carefully. "I can't really tell you every detail. These photos are part of Jane's new idea. It's too complicated to explain here, but there's no reason Ned should have these."

C.D. walked over to Jane's workstation.

He clicked to open a file on her computer screen and the same row of photos appeared. "Ned must have copied her files," he said.

"He was spying on Jane at the Brass Horn Restaurant," Benny blurted out before anyone could stop him. "We saw him spying when we were hiding behind our menus."

"Benny!" Jessie interrupted. "We don't really know what was going on, C.D. All of us were just having lunch today at the Brass Horn, and so were Jane and Ned."

"What?" C.D. said, his voice rising. "Jane is in Hampstead. She left a couple hours ago. As for Ned, I sent him over to your place to drop off a new computer mouse that works better with *Ringmaster II*. Then I asked him to run some errands for me. Of course, he can go anywhere he wants for lunch, so I guess he did."

"So that's why Ned was at our house today," said Benny. "He came to our door, but Watch started barking, then Ned went away."

C.D. smiled. "Well, Ned gets kind of grouchy with the way I run QuestMaster, what with dogs and kids and all. And he didn't want to go to your house in the first place."

"How long has Ned been at QuestMaster?" Henry asked.

"Since before there even was a Quest-Master," C.D. said. "I brought him over from another computer company. And when I realized how good Andy was with computers, I asked him to work for us, too. Ned's always been the one with the big ideas," C.D. continued. "Now Jane is coming up with some amazing things to do with our games. But it looks like Ned is spying on Jane's work."

The dogs began barking. They raced to the hallway. A door banged.

Ned Porter walked in, carrying a pile of boxes. "Call the dogs away, if you don't mind," he said to C.D. and the Aldens in a grouchy voice. "Is this an office or a dog pound?"

"Both!" C.D. said.

If C.D. hoped this would make Ned smile, he was wrong. Ned set the boxes down on a nearby table. He gave one of them to the Aldens. "I was supposed to give you this new computer mouse this morning, but that dog of yours chased me away."

"It's because you ran away," Benny said. "Once Watch meets most people, he's friendly."

"I came back to get a few things from my desk before I head home," Ned told C.D. "I've been fooling around with some new things on my home computer."

C.D. paused before he spoke. "Anything you want to share with the staff, Ned?"

"Nope," Ned replied. He stuffed the photos on his desk into a folder and headed for the door.

"Had lunch yet?" C.D. asked.

Same answer. "Nope," he said, then he left the studio.

C.D. shook his head. "I'm going to have a private talk with Ned about those photos and about the 'Head Shots' file. I hoped he'd tell me on his own, but no such luck.

And he lied about having lunch, too. I don't know what I can say about that."

Violet looked a little upset. "Maybe Ned didn't lie about lunch. He was just standing in the restaurant right behind Jane Driver and the two people she was with."

C.D. straightened up. "What two people? Do you remember what they looked like, Violet?"

Violet wasn't sure.

"I remember," Benny said. "I think one was tall with a bushy beard."

C.D.'s face went pale. "A man with a beard and . . . was the other man bald?"

"We couldn't tell," said Benny. "He was wearing a hat."

"I hope they don't turn out to be who I think they are," said C.D.

"Who?" Henry asked.

C.D. looked upset. "They're two people I used to work with a few years back. Now they've founded a game company, too. It's called Comet Interactive Games. We went our separate ways when I discovered I couldn't trust them."

"Do you trust us?" Benny asked. "We were hiding behind our menus and spying in the restaurant."

C.D. smiled a little. "Everybody enjoys people-watching in restaurants, Benny. I think that's okay if you don't stare or make them uncomfortable."

"They didn't see us," Benny continued. "Then lunch came, and that was more fun. And now we're here."

C.D. thought about this. "Yes, you're all here. Now I wish Jane were here, too. I need to get to the bottom of this."

CHAPTER 7

The Computer Talks Back

Grandfather and Mrs. Mc-Gregor were back home when the children returned from QuestMaster.

"I read your note about your meeting at QuestMaster," Grandfather said to the children. "So how did Watch do on his first day of work?"

"Watch took a long doggie break instead of a coffee break," Henry said, trying to look serious. "C.D. isn't sure he wants to hire Watch unless he learns how to type with his paws."

Grandfather and Mrs. McGregor laughed at the thought of Watch sitting at the computer instead of under it.

"Seriously, though," Henry continued, "there wasn't any meeting. C.D. thought someone at the studio was playing a prank on us."

"You know, I wondered about this meeting," Mrs. McGregor said, "since Andy Porter came by again while you were gone. It seemed odd that he wouldn't be at the meeting, too. Since he worked on the computer before, I let him in. Oh, dear, I hope there isn't a problem."

Jessie felt sorry for Mrs. McGregor. She was only trying to help. "That's okay. We were having a bit of trouble with the computer. Now maybe Andy fixed it. Thanks."

The computer was still on in the den.

"Gee, why is the *Ringmaster II* screen on if Andy was working on the network?" Jessie asked.

Henry tried to check his e-mail, but the QuestMaster network still didn't work. "I guess Andy didn't have any luck. Now, I wonder why he booted up *Ringmaster II*."

Henry hit the start button. The Magician came on-screen. "I'm not going to play a real game," Henry said. "I just want to try a few things, like finding Nadje again. When we were with C.D., I was beginning to think we imagined her."

"There she is, Henry," Soo Lee said when she saw the two-faced woman again.

"Good. I guess our minds weren't playing tricks after all," Jessie said, looking on.

An amazing thing happened when Henry slid the computer mouse over to Jessie. When she mistakenly brushed the right button on the mouse key, a message came out of Nadje's mouth. Henry read it to the others:

"*I need to discuss the situation as soon as possible. Let's meet at 3:00 Tuesday. I just hope no one follows me.*"

"What does that mean?" Soo Lee asked her cousins. "Is Nadje a real person? Is she going to come over here?"

Henry sat back in his chair. "Something is definitely going on that isn't part of *Ringmaster II*. Part of a real message got mixed up with the game."

"This is getting spooky," Soo Lee said.

Violet put her arms around Soo Lee and Benny. Soo Lee was right. This game was getting spooky. The computer seemed to be giving the Aldens messages somehow!

"Okay, there's Arthur, the older boy character," Jessie said. "He's watching Nadje chase the Magician, and he looks really worried."

"Let's see if Arthur has any spells to rescue the Magician," Henry said. When Henry clicked on the boy's saddlebag, a stone fell to the ground and a message appeared.

Violet read the words:

"Now the son must save the father,
So use the spell to help another.
Nadje's watching, so take care,
To use the stone that's fallen there."

Before the Aldens had time to use the computer mouse, Nadje grabbed the stone.

"Should we call C.D. and have him come over to see what's going on with this game?" Henry said. "He didn't even know about Nadje."

"Not yet," Jessie answered. "I have a funny feeling this game is just for us."

"The only character who can move now is Arthur," Violet noted. "He must be the one who has to save the Magician." The children studied the screen for clues.

Benny noticed a fountain by the side of the road. "Maybe the fountain has magic water. But be careful in case the water is poison like in the other game."

Like Benny, Soo Lee had sharp eyes. "Look, there are birds drinking the water and flying around. That probably means it's safe to drink."

When Violet clicked on the fountain, the children heard the tinkling sound of water on the computer speaker. This meant the boy, Arthur, could drink the water.

"The water's safe!" Henry said. "Good

for you for figuring that out. Maybe you can even figure out how to help him get the magic stone away from Nadje."

Jessie had some ideas. "Can I try? I have a feeling Arthur is the key to freeing the Magician from Nadje."

Because of the many odd sounds coming from the computer speaker, the children barely heard the phone ring.

Finally Henry realized the ringing sound was coming from the hallway, not the computer speaker. He raced to answer the phone. The children heard him talking to someone.

"That was C.D.," Henry said when he returned to the den. "He's curious about how we're doing with the game, but he won't have time to meet today. He said he's driving up to Hampstead to get the special chip Jane was supposed to pick up. It turns out she never showed up. And know what else? He can't find Ned or Andy, either."

"Did you tell him about all the strange things happening in *Ringmaster II*?" Violet asked.

Henry shook his head. "Not yet. I want to figure out a few things on our own first. But he said there's a meeting tomorrow when he gets back. He wants everybody there. Let's talk with him then."

"Sure thing. Hey, you know what?" Jessie asked. "We're not getting anywhere with this game right now. Why don't we go into town and pick up a copy of Fix-It software so we can fix the network?"

Henry agreed. "Good idea, Jessie. I'll shut down *Ringmaster II*."

"Wait! Not yet!" Benny cried. "Look at the water fountain again. Doesn't it look just like the one on Old Post Road?"

The other children stared at the screen.

"You know what? You're right, Benny," Jessie said. "It's a copy of the stone fountain they used to use for horses in the days before cars — the one on the road between Greenfield and Burrville."

"Can we go see it? Maybe it's a clue. Please? Please?" Benny begged.

"And what about the 'three o'clock' message that came out of Nadje's mouth?" said

Violet. "Maybe that is part of the clue, too!"

Jessie agreed. "You could be right, Violet. Let's be at the fountain at three. We can walk. It's only about a mile away. We'll stop by Computer City on the way back."

Henry shut down the game. "I suppose the fountain *could* be some kind of clue in the game. Or else the designers are copying stuff from around Greenfield, like the Brass Horn or this fountain, just because they like it."

Benny was ready for an adventure. "Now we can be in the game, too."

CHAPTER 8

A Mysterious Fountain

The children set out to find the old drinking fountain on Old Post Road. As they walked along, cars whizzed by in both directions. Gas stations, stores, and office buildings lined the busy road.

"Grandfather said when he was a little boy, farmers and peddlers still drove their horse carts along this road," Violet said. "I guess the fountain is the only landmark left from those days."

Along the way, the children passed the Big Dipper, their favorite ice-cream stand.

Benny licked his lips. "Can we stop for ice cream on the way back? I might be hungry by then."

"*Might* be hungry?" Henry asked, laughing.

A few minutes later, the Aldens spotted the fountain up ahead. Clumps of roadside daisies and overgrown grasses nearly covered the old landmark. It hadn't been used as a watering stop for travelers for many years.

Soo Lee wrinkled her nose when she looked down into the fountain. "The old rainwater is all yucky and green."

Henry walked around the fountain. "Why would anybody include this old thing in a computer game? It's all covered over with moss and weeds."

"I think it's pretty," Violet said. "Maybe there's some other reason it was in the game. Let's look around."

"What does that sign say?" Soo Lee asked a few minutes later. She pointed to a nearby sign no one else had spotted.

" 'Comet Interactive Games,' " Jessie answered. "That's the name of the company C.D. told us about — the one with those two people he doesn't trust. Let's follow that side road where the sign is pointing."

The Comet Interactive Games building was set way back from Old Post Road, up a hill and past some trees.

"You can't really tell that the building is here," Henry said. "Uh-oh. There's a gate. I don't think we can go inside."

Sure enough, a security guard came over. "You kids have business here?" he asked in a sharp voice.

"Sort of. We're curious to find out if this is where Comet Interactive Games are made," Jessie said truthfully.

This information didn't make the guard any friendlier. "You and a hundred other kids pestering us all the time," he said. "You need an appointment to go inside."

Jessie and Henry motioned for the other children to head back down the hill.

"Sorry," Henry said. "We didn't know."

"Well, now you do," the guard said.

"He didn't like us," Soo Lee said as the

children walked away. "Can we go home now?"

As they walked along the side of the driveway, the Aldens heard a car coming up fast from behind. Henry and Jessie pulled the younger children behind some bushes.

A white convertible whizzed past. A woman with a ponytail was driving.

"Did you see that? It had a QuestMaster parking sticker on the bumper," Jessie said after the car went by. "I could have sworn that was Jane Driver at the wheel."

A minute later, the children saw a green car pull onto the road from a clump of trees. It followed the convertible down the hill. Like the white convertible, this one had a QuestMaster parking sticker on its bumper. Only this time the children were positive who the driver was.

"That's Ned Porter's car!" Henry said. "I'm sure of it. He must have been visiting the Comet Interactive offices, too. Only why did he park in the woods?"

Jessie thought about this. "Do you think

he and Jane are up to no good? Now we really have to figure out what's going on, so we can tell C.D."

From where they were standing, the children could see all the way down to Old Post Road. They noticed that the green car followed the white convertible at a distance until the Aldens couldn't see either car anymore.

Henry stepped ahead of the other children. "Let's leave a message for C.D. about this as soon as we get home."

"Do we still have time for ice cream?" Benny asked when he saw the Big Dipper ice-cream stand up ahead.

Jessie took Benny's hand. "We always have time for ice cream."

When the children entered the Big Dipper, there was only one customer inside. As the Aldens got closer, they realized who it was.

"Andy Porter!" Henry whispered. "Of all people."

Andy held a cone in one hand, but it was

dripping all over, as if he'd forgotten he was holding it.

"How many times have you seen that white convertible go by here?" the Aldens overheard Andy ask the girl behind the counter.

"I told you, I don't know," the girl answered impatiently. "Why do you keep coming here and asking me all these questions about that car?"

Andy tapped on the metal counter nervously. "I just need to know, that's all. Have you seen that woman around here with a bearded man and a bald man?"

"A few times." The girl looked over Andy's head at the Aldens. "Look, I can't talk right now. Some other customers just came in. May I help you?"

Andy whirled around. When he saw the Aldens, he seemed to want to speak to them. But he stopped himself, nodded quickly as a way of saying good-bye, and left. The Aldens saw him race off on his bike, which had been parked outside.

"May I help you?" the ice-cream girl repeated, this time louder.

"What was that all about?" Henry asked the girl.

"Do you know him?" the girl asked. "He's been in here a bunch of times. He's always wanting to know about some people who work at Comet Interactive Games up the road."

"The woman in the white convertible?" Jessie asked.

The girl nodded.

"What about a tall man who looks like that boy?" Henry asked. "He's got a green car."

The girl shook her head. She was tired of all these nosy customers. "Look, I'm just here to serve ice cream, not spy on people or watch what cars go in and out of the parking lot. Now, if you want to order, please tell me what you want."

The Aldens ordered their cones and went outside to eat them.

"Why did Andy leave so fast when he saw

us?" Benny asked. "He didn't even finish his cone. But I'm going to finish mine."

Benny and Soo Lee licked up every last drip.

While he was finishing, Benny picked up a piece of paper blowing near his feet.

"What does that say?" Soo Lee wanted to know.

"Boring stuff, like a list or something," Benny said. "Let's see. What's that word, Violet?" he asked when he got stuck.

" 'Nadje — three o'clock!' " Violet answered. "Why would Nadje's name be on this piece of paper?" She grabbed the paper from Benny and ran over to Jessie and Henry with it. "It also says, 'Check Head Shots.' Didn't C.D. say 'Head Shots' had something to do with Jane's computer idea?"

"Now we'd really better get a move on," Henry said. "I have a feeling Andy dropped that paper when he raced off. This is getting stranger and stranger all the time."

Jessie hurried the younger children along.

"Don't forget. We still have to pick up the Fix-It program at the computer store before we go home. Maybe that will help us figure out what's going on inside our computer."

"I hope we can figure out what's going on outside our computer, too," Benny added.

CHAPTER 9

Listening In

The Aldens and Soo Lee didn't waste any time getting to Computer City. They passed aisles of games without stopping to check the brightly colored boxes. They were in a hurry.

Henry went straight to the shelves of software designed to fix computer problems.

"That sign says, '*Ringmaster II* Coming Soon,' " Benny said. "It came to our house already."

A young man in a red shirt came over.

"May I help you?"

"Do you have the Fix-It program?" Henry asked. "We're having some problems with a computer network we're on. I heard that Fix-It can help."

The man handed a Fix-It box to Henry. "Here you go. Anything else?"

"No, but thanks," Henry said. "Well, I do have one question. Are there any games where players somehow use photos to make up their own characters?"

The man laughed. "Whoever figures out how to make that idea work is going to be a millionaire. I've heard rumors that a couple of companies are trying something like that out — using a scanner to put photos of real people or places in a game to make it more realistic and fun. Of course, the photo-faces will move and change expression, too. Right now, I don't think anybody has figured out exactly how a player can do that at home."

The Aldens tried to hide their excitement. They had a feeling someone they knew was getting pretty close to figuring out exactly how to do that.

"Thanks," Henry said to the salesman. "Okay, everybody, let's go pay for this."

There was a long line at the checkout counter. While Henry waited, the other children browsed through a display of new games. While they were reading the game boxes, they overheard a familiar voice talking loudly in the next aisle. It sounded like the person was talking on the phone.

"It doesn't matter that it won't work," a woman's voice said. "I just have to show up with something. When it doesn't work, that will give us more time."

Jessie put her finger to her lips when she noticed Benny was about to say something. "Shhh," she whispered. "Let's go." Benny took Soo Lee's hand and they started walking.

After the Aldens left the store, Benny blurted out to Henry what he had been holding in. "Jane Driver was in the store, but she didn't see us."

Henry was amazed. "Everywhere we go, she goes."

"Never mind that," Jessie said. "Everywhere she goes, Ned Porter goes, too. There's his green car in the corner of the parking lot."

The Aldens waved several times at Ned. First he ignored them. Then he started his car and left the parking lot in a hurry.

When the children got home, they saw a familiar blue bicycle leaning against the picket fence.

"Isn't that Andy's bike?" Benny asked as they went inside through the kitchen door. "I'm going to give him that piece of paper he dropped."

"Shhh," Jessie said. "Let's wait to see what he says first. I want to find out why he keeps coming over here."

Mrs. McGregor spied the Computer City bag Henry was carrying. "Another computer bag?" she said. "Your friend Andy just went into the den with a bag from that

store. I hope you didn't both buy the same thing."

"I sure hope not, Mrs. McGregor," Henry said.

When Andy saw the children come into the den, he clicked off the screen he'd been working on. He picked up a Computer City bag and pulled out his own Fix-It software box.

"Wait!" Henry said, holding up his own bag. "We just bought the same program. I think we can take over now. You must have a lot of other things to do at QuestMaster."

Andy seemed very nervous. "Well, this morning C.D. said to come over anyway."

Henry looked at Andy for a long time. "Are you sure? He told us he was going to the city to get a special chip Jane was supposed to get."

Andy's face grew pale. "What are you talking about?"

Henry decided to be mysterious. "Nothing we can talk about. Now maybe you can tell us why you left so fast when we ran into you at the Big Dipper. And why you're here again."

Andy swallowed hard before he answered. "I told you. I'm supposed to help get the network going from your computer."

Henry was usually pretty easygoing, but not today. "Well, this is our computer now, and we need to learn how to fix it ourselves. Thanks for offering to help, but don't bother installing the Fix-It program. We'll use our own."

Benny tugged on Jessie's hand. He showed her the crumpled paper he'd picked up at the ice-cream stand. Jessie shook her head as if to say no.

Too late. Andy spotted the paper. He blushed. "Where'd you get that? I was looking for it. I have some notes on there that I need. I guess I dropped it — by mistake, of course."

Jessie stepped in front of Benny. "Hold on a second, Andy. Tell us what's on it first. Maybe it doesn't belong to you."

"It's an appointment I wrote down that

Jane had at three o'clock today," he said, reaching for the paper.

Jessie pulled it away. "But that's not exactly what it says. It must belong to someone else."

With five pairs of eyes staring at him, Andy Porter knew the Aldens weren't handing over that note. He turned and left.

After she heard the door close, Jessie read the note. "Andy was wrong. He said the name was Jane, but it says Nadje."

Henry put down the Fix-It box he was about to open. "Wait a minute. Repeat what you just said."

Jessie wrinkled her forehead. "Okay. The name on this paper is Nadje. . . . Hmmm. *Nadje* looks an awful lot like *Jane*. It has the same letters plus the first letter of her last name — *D*."

"But Nadje is a two-faced witch," Benny said, "and Jane is just a regular person."

"Maybe Jane *is* two-faced!" Jessie said excitedly. "Maybe she acts one way at Quest-Master but another way . . ." Her voice trailed off.

She turned to Henry. "Didn't C.D. say he was having a meeting tomorrow?"

Henry nodded.

"Okay. Here's what we do," Jessie went on. "Let's bring this computer to the office. We'll say we were having problems with it and ask Jane, Ned, and Andy to help us out. There's something about our *Ringmaster II* program that *is* different. I have a feeling one of those people knows what it is."

CHAPTER 10

The Aldens Set a Trap

After breakfast the next day, the children were pleased to learn that Grandfather was also going to the QuestMaster meeting. C.D. had invited his uncle John and Mr. Alden to take a peek at *Ringmaster II*.

Grandfather, Violet, and Soo Lee sat waiting in the front seat of the station wagon while Jessie and Henry packed the computer into the back.

"I can't quite imagine working at a place like QuestMaster," Grandfather said. "When I started out in business we all had to wear suits and starched white shirts. There certainly were no dogs at the office."

"And I bet you didn't play basketball with your boss, either," said Violet.

"No, I didn't." Grandfather laughed. "Though it might have been more fun if I had." Grandfather turned to the back of the station wagon. "Are we all set back there?" he asked Jessie and Henry.

"Almost," Jessie answered. She shut the back door of the station wagon and she and Henry came around to the side door and slid in next to Benny.

"Ready," said Henry.

Grandfather started the car. "What a shame the new computer is giving you so much trouble," he said over the sound of the engine.

"I have a feeling that we're going to give someone *else* trouble with our computer," Henry whispered to Jessie. "Not the other way around."

The Aldens arrived early for the Quest-Master meeting. Henry and Jessie set up the computer at an empty workstation next to

Jane's. In no time, they had it up and running. They booted up *Ringmaster II*. This time they knew for sure they would have no trouble finding Nadje, the old stone fountain, or the Brass Horn sign inside their game.

One by one, the designers arrived at work.

When C.D. saw the children, he came over to greet them. He noticed their computer right away. "Still having problems with the network? Andy told me he took care of everything the other day."

Just at that moment, Ned arrived and heard his son's name. "Andy's coming soon. You looking for him?"

"Hi, Ned," C.D. answered. "Yes, see if you and Andy can help me figure out the problems the Aldens are still having."

Ned didn't look too pleased about this. "You said we had an important meeting today to discuss *Ringmaster II*. Andy came in especially — "

Hearing his name when he walked by,

Andy stopped. "You need me, Dad? I was . . . Oh, hi," he said in a lower voice to the Aldens. His eyes widened when he noticed the Aldens' computer. "Why did you bring that here?" He looked at C.D. nervously. "I offered to fix it yesterday, but Henry told me not to."

C.D. was completely confused now. What was going on? "Did you send Andy away?" he asked the Aldens.

Before the children could answer, Ned interrupted. "Seems as if we're wasting a lot of time on one computer for kids who don't even work here." He looked at his watch. "Just about everybody's here. Can't this wait?"

"Ned," C.D. said in a low voice, "I'll decide when we'll start the meeting. The Aldens brought their machine in for a reason. Before we try to monkey around with the network problems, I want everybody to take a look at their copy of *Ringmaster II*."

Andy stepped away. "Um . . . I have some last-minute stuff I, uh . . . have to check for the computers you're shipping out to the high school, C.D., so I'd better go."

"That can wait, Andy," C.D. said. "The Aldens told me about some interesting things that showed up in their game. You're such a computer whiz, I think you should stick around." C.D. looked over Andy's head and saw Jane come into the studio.

She started to turn away when she saw everyone staring at her. "I forgot something in my car," she said. "I'll be right back."

C.D. forced a tense laugh. "I must be wearing my mean boss face today. Everybody's acting as if they have someplace else they'd rather be. Jane, I want to show you something interesting here. Now."

Jane knew she had no choice. C.D. was the boss.

When Mr. Alden and John Romer saw the group huddled around the Aldens, they wanted to get in on the excitement, too.

"Okay," Henry began. "I already booted up *Ringmaster II*."

A new screen came on, and Nadje appeared.

"Look what happens when we click on to this two-faced woman," Jessie said. "Her name is Nadje, and she's only on our copy of *Ringmaster II*."

The Aldens looked around at everyone. They could hardly wait for Henry to click the mouse.

"Watch the screen, Andy," Ned said to his son in a sharp voice.

Andy didn't respond. He wasn't watching the screen because he was too busy watching Jane Driver.

Jane seemed to shrink away. "Why is everyone staring at me?" she asked in a dry, whispery voice. "That two-headed character isn't me, if that's what you're all thinking."

Jessie found the wrinkled note in her backpack and handed it to C.D. "Andy dropped this yesterday, and we found it. He wrote down a meeting time, but instead of writing down Jane's name, he wrote Nadje's name instead."

Everyone turned to Andy.

Andy turned away from everyone. Then he began to speak. "Jessie's right. Nadje is a character I designed in the Aldens' game. I meant for the character to be like Jane — two-faced. The Aldens figured it all out the way I planned, but I didn't want my dad to find out I was leaving all the clues."

C.D. shook his head. "Clues to what, Andy?"

Andy faced everyone. He swallowed hard. "There are *two* things we found out about Jane. First, my dad and I found out that Jane stole his idea for Head Shots."

"Head Shots?" C.D. asked in an angry voice. "How could that be your idea, Ned? I know you haven't been happy with some of the things that go on here, but accusing a new employee of theft, then getting your son to trap her? That's not the way we do things at QuestMaster."

Andy stepped forward before Ned could say anything. "No! No! You've got it wrong,

C.D. My dad never asked me to do anything. He wanted credit for his idea, but Jane showed it to you first. We even had fights about this. I knew it wasn't fair for Jane to get credit for his idea. I wanted Dad to tell you, but he wouldn't. And he made me promise not to tell you. We didn't have proof. That's why I planted clues in the Aldens' computer. I wanted *them* to follow the clues and figure out what Jane was really up to. You said the Alden kids were good detectives. I thought if *they* found out the truth about Jane, you would believe it."

C.D. looked at Jane and then turned back to Ned and Andy. "And just what is Jane really up to, Andy?"

"She went to Comet Interactive Games in her white car," Benny interrupted excitedly. "We all saw her."

"What?" exclaimed C.D. "Jane went to Comet Interactive?"

The Aldens nodded. "We followed the clues in *Ringmaster II* to the stone fountain on Old Post Road, and we saw her drive from their parking lot," said Jessie.

"That's right," said Andy. "First she stole my father's idea, then she took it to Comet Interactive. And now we have witnesses besides ourselves."

Jessie wondered about something. "There's something I don't get, Andy. Why did you run away from us at the ice-cream stand? We could have shared all this right there — the note, the meeting, everything. We weren't a hundred percent sure who was up to no good, but we were close. That's why we brought our computer in."

"Sorry I ran away," Andy said. "I was afraid Jane would see us together and figure out we knew something."

C.D. was so upset he needed a minute to gather his thoughts. "Jane, did you go to Comet Interactive Games with Head Shots — Ned's game, as it turns out?"

Before Jane could answer, Andy interrupted. "Just read this," Andy said. He sat at the keyboard and clicked on Nadje. The message that came out of Nadje's mouth appeared on-screen.

I need to discuss the situation as soon as possible. Let's meet at 3:00 Tuesday. I just hope no one follows me.

Andy looked directly at C.D. "This came from an e-mail Jane sent. She accidentally left some e-mail on her old computer, then you gave it to the Aldens. So I stuck it in the game, hoping the Aldens would follow Jane to Comet Interactive Games, then tell you. Jane's e-mail is QuestMaster property. Just check her mailbox."

By this time Jane had slipped away to her own computer. C.D. and the Aldens weren't far behind.

"Don't even think about erasing anything," C.D. said from behind Jane. "Just open the e-mail Andy's talking about."

Instead of obeying, Jane sank back into her chair. "I don't have to. You're going to fire me anyway. I used to work at Comet Interactive Games. The people there never listened to my ideas. They were working on the photo idea, too — that players could create characters in a game from personal photos. But they weren't making any progress with it. Then I came to QuestMaster and found out Ned was working on the same thing."

Jane turned to Ned. "Sorry, Ned. You always left your computer on without a screensaver to cover up your screen. I saw the name 'Head Shots' and photos on your desk. I heard you call Andy 'Dandy Andy' a few times, so I guessed that was your password. After that, getting into your computer was easy."

Ned banged his fist down on Jane's desk. "Well, good riddance to you and Comet Interactive Games. Head Shots is our project. And I know what it needs to make it work. Now you can all quit snooping around and we can get to work."

"But you were snooping, too," Jessie said to Ned.

"Okay, I admit it," Ned said. "I followed

Jane everywhere. Meanwhile, without my knowing it, my son here was trying to save his own dad."

"Just like in the game!" Soo Lee cried. "The boy, Arthur, tries to save the Magician from Nadje."

C.D. was confused by all this information, but he knew one thing for sure. "Jane, you can go back to Comet Interactive Games. You are no longer employed at my company. As for Head Shots, Ned, it's not going to be as hard as you think. QuestMaster has a million dollars and a couple geniuses in you and Andy."

After Jane cleaned out her desk and left, Benny saw Ned's camera on the computer table. "Hey, Ned, can you take our pictures? You could put us in *Ringmaster III*."

Ned picked up the camera. Watch barked. The Aldens stood together. Benny said, "*Cheese*."

"There," said Ned as he snapped the picture, and for the first time the Aldens saw him smile.

"I think we may want to design a whole new game for this Head Shots feature," C.D. said.

Everyone watched as the photo zipped out of the camera and slowly developed before their eyes.

"What will you call your new game?" Benny asked.

Andy put a hand on Benny's shoulder. "In honor of the Aldens, how about "Mystery-Masters I?"

And everyone laughed and cheered.

GERTRUDE CHANDLER WARNER discovered when she was teaching that many readers who like an exciting story could find no books that were both easy and fun to read. She decided to try to meet this need, and her first book, *The Boxcar Children*, quickly proved she had succeeded.

Miss Warner drew on her own experiences to write the mystery. As a child she spent hours watching trains go by on the tracks opposite her family home. She often dreamed about what it would be like to set up housekeeping in a caboose or freight car — the situation the Alden children find themselves in.

When Miss Warner received requests for more adventures involving Henry, Jessie, Violet, and Benny Alden, she began additional stories. In each, she chose a special setting and introduced unusual or eccentric characters who liked the unpredictable.

While the mystery element is central to each of Miss Warner's books, she never thought of them as strictly juvenile mysteries. She liked to stress the Aldens' independence and resourcefulness and their solid New England devotion to using up and making do. The Aldens go about most of their adventures with as little adult supervision as possible — something else that delights young readers.

Miss Warner lived in Putnam, Connecticut, until her death in 1979. During her lifetime, she received hundreds of letters from girls and boys telling her how much they liked her books.